The Ohio State University Press/*The Journal* Award in Poetry

American Husband

Kary Wayson

THE OHIO STATE UNIVERSITY PRESS · COLUMBUS

Library of Congress Cataloging-in-Publication data
Wayson, Kary, 1970–
American husband / Kary Wayson.
p. cm.
Includes bibliographical references.
"Winner of the 2008 Ohio State University Press/The journal award in poetry."
Summary: A volume of poetry about motherhood, travel, being.
ISBN-13: 978-0-8142-5159-1 (pbk. : alk. paper)
ISBN-10: 0-8142-5159-5 (pbk. : alk. paper)
ISBN-13: 978-0-8142-9210-5 (cd-rom)
1. American poetry—21st century. I. Title.
PS3623.A985A85 2009
811'.6—dc22
2009026667

This book is available in the following editions:
Paper (ISBN 978-0-8142-5159-1)
CD-ROM (ISBN 978-0-8142-9210-5)

Cover design by Mia Risberg
Text design by Juliet Williams
Type set in ITC Legacy Serif
Printed by BookMobile, Inc.

∞ The paper used in this publication meets the minimum requirements of the American National Standard for Information Sciences—Permanence of Paper for Printed Library Materials. ANSI Z.39.48-1992.

9 8 7 6 5 4 3 2 1

American Husband

O, Empty-of-Hours, the doctor's a clock. His hand
is a serrated knife. Heavy his books, his
medical meanings,

his pharmacological eyes.

Father Infallible, Doctor Indelible, Goat
you've got, my goad-You, and your mal-
practice suits, your wingtips and tuxedoes.

Doctor Parenthesis, Father
for emphasis, Stepmothers Must
and Because: Doctor dismiss
my dire diagnosis—my god's

a blot—of implausible pause.

Dear Doctor, Dear Proctor, ad-
Minister my test (Your office assigns
your affections.) Dear Doctor, Dear

Forceps, my Father, forget this—
I'll ration your attention.

I'll wait
and I'll wait. I'll compile
and I'll plate
an unending compendium of
juvenile complaints:

American make me, American take me
with you when you go. You do not do, you do not do—
Faster, Bastard! American
Fetch! *you do not do*—you don't.

American Father, My General Boss
I am your lather—and you
are my loss. Professor my lecture, mother
my tongue—I live
with a desk where nothing gets done.
Inhibit my habits and dress me in gauze—my god's
a clot. Of unsolvable cause.

American Husband, American Head, nobody
stopped me, nobody said *Surgeons*
must be very careful/ When they take the knife!

CONTENTS

ACKNOWLEDGMENTS

Many thanks to the journals and anthologies in which the following poems, some in earlier versions, first appeared:

Alaska Quarterly Review: "Flu Song in Spanish," "Echolocution"
Best American Poetry 2007: "Flu Song in Spanish"
Borderlands: Texas Poetry Review: "Hard Feelings," "The Curtains Are Another Kind of Husband"
Boston Review: "American Husband"
Cranky: "Quid Pro," "Regret Red," and "Can Be Jackets, Can Be Bees"
Crab Creek Review: "Because Because"
FIELD: "Good God," "Fever with Guitars," "The Chief," "Snarcissus," "Love Is Not a Word," and "Poppies"
Filter: "The Four Corners of Fifth & Lenora" and "Untitled Manifesto"
KNOCK: "Chicken"
LitRag: "If English," "Cruelty Made Me," and "The Wrong Place for a Long Time"
Mass. Ave.: "More of the Same"
Poets on Painters: "Intimacy Vs. Autonomy"
Rivet: "Federico & Garcia"
Shade 2006: An Anthology of Poetry and Fiction: "Pick It Up Again"
The Journal: "Double Down" and "I Turn My Silence Over"
The Nation: "The Mean Time"
The Rendezvous Reader: Northwest Writing: "Each Foot as Feet Should"

Thank you to Trisha, and to Kevin, and to Rob, and to Jessica. Thanks Erin, thanks Martha, thanks Shannon and Rebecca. Thanks to the Espy Foundation, for the time, and to Artist Trust, for the money. Thanks to AJ for the Dog. And to Kathy Fagan, for picking mine—and me! To Dad, thanks for everything. And Olena: like a tree! You're magic. Kary.

The Four Corners of Fifth & Lenora

I timed my arrival to make an X.
At the intersection you were on the other side.
I smiled like the city bus between us.
A sick, fluorescent smile.
In that moment my coat blew open:
half-slip hiked around my waist,
my hair I hoped a wave of grain. This
is not a weekend feeling.
I am holding my heart against my chest.
In the city of just me you made me like a guest
and I gave you how many tries.

More of the Same

But even with my mouth on your thigh
I want my mouth on your thigh.
At the center bite of bread I want the whole loaf
toasted, and an orange. On a sunny day
I want more sun, more skin for the weather.
I'm in Seattle wishing for Seattle,
for this walk along the water, for her hand while I hold it:
I want to tie my wrist to a red balloon.
I'm counting my tips.
I'm counting the tips I could have made.
I want the television on, the television off.
In the ocean, I want to float an inch above it
and when my father finally held me
like a stripe of seaweed over his wet arm,
I was kicking to get away, wishing he'd hold me
like he held me while I was kicking away. Listen to me.
I want to leave when I'm walking out the door.

Cruelty Made Me

Love came along and said what: *What?*
without even a single word.
Said *wait* by the far side of the river
and *when* by the black limb of the crow tree
growing through my kitchen window.

Love came along and said *let me*
(and let me say she'd let me)
but cruelty made me
with my back turned. Grew me
according to a twisted line of light
so I've grown twisted, like the light,
shaped
like a staircase
and run with a long red rug.

Love came along and flashed me her badge,
said her name rhymes with *test*
and keeps to the meter of bare legs
in a loose dress. But cruelty made love sleepless
and sleepless, made me cruel:
each tooth in the tracks
of all my zippers latched, belts all
buckled and button
by button, I'm done.

Snarcissus

Pretty thing, to have gotten you by the bulb collar
tonight, in limp lamp light—to demonstrate your neck
with my thumbs.
Any transparency tries what light there is this late.
Tries it like you try my patience. Wears it
like you wear a dress: skinny skirt
stitched to your skinny hips, the frill
to the bodice of the bloom.
Silly thing, to feel
disheveled in front of a flower.
The sun set you up on the west-most crest
of a city divided by two hills.
I am embarrassed here, dirty
in a clean chair, my hair
like someone took a steak knife to the piano. Still,
I can say I've known you well and I will.
My hindsight possesses the sense
of your smell. A wedding dress in a cedar chest so
there—you happy?

Regret Red

This is slow going, this paling
of what's worse than purple
into some dumb lesser version
of lavender or black:
a much less lustrous pick
of what could be called my color
if I were better bred. Red,

as if regret were in love with love
and rejected it,
bound the bare foot I kicked hard
through your guitar until it bled
blood red, as if I were a river running
on my river bed.

I choose the hours between dread
and dread, when I'm free
from feeling anything, like an extra finger
I forget and remember. Regret

as a red crab holed up in a hot rock
half in and half out and *goddammit*
cursing quite a bit, that word *worse*
irritating the inside of his hot head.

Red as a red car
irrevocably in reverse
on a day that drives away without a back bumper.
That moment: as many times as I can make it. The black fabric
of the convertible top pleated in a neat pile
in front of the trunk as if

regret were the age
my daughter would be.
Red as a bee-keeper's face.
Red like a lot of things.

Poppies

Hair in the brushes, in the bread bag, snagged
in my bracelet

and clogging the kitchen drain. Your hair
and how it hangs, your face and how it falls

—your throat, how thick: your feet. Your fuse.

Your body and my body and the mark on the wall above the bed—
one crow

sticks

and cracks—a black sip from a flask. How the grass
grows geese

from a goose. Water

and the way it floats
the gulls and bugs

and boats. Your will and what I want—
which words when, where, and whether or not
I'm home.

You've got me ringing like a neighbor's telephone.

Echolocution

I am at home. I am
interviewing the telephone. She says hello

when I say hello: Hello.
The front doorknob fits against a gauge in the wall.

I cough and stop and scratch and stop and listen—
when I listen for long enough I'm lost.

Voices of men recite the radio news. Time
is a travel advertisement.

I hang on to the telephone like a handle.
Fastened to the wood wall of a boat.

She says what I say while I say it.
When I listen for long enough I'm lost.

The light's got rice in it, like after a wedding:
me in my ambulance, you in yours.

The Embolus

Time's ear
is infected. It itches
and hatches
a pocket.
She turned herself out.

I was sixteen
when she miscarried.
I met her

four doctors. She harrowed herself
a hole from a scratch. They scraped and they sucked
and I coughed it all up. My mouth
is a basket of examples.

Time's ear
is inflected. It pitches
and catches
a ladder.
She pulled herself out.

She looks like I look–
but I'm getting older. She harrowed herself
whole from a patch. God Himself
must have glanced away

when she was digging around in her purse for a match.

I Turn My Silence Over

I am in the tenth month of the ninth life
of my silence.
My baby's grown fat enough to feed me.
I turn my silence over. I turn it
towards my mother. It wears
the expressionless face of an oscillating fan.

Each day, at intervals, a bell brings
enormous horses to the middle of my alphabet.
I turn my silence over.
I'm not speaking to my mother.
My mute has balloons for hands.

O Underbite!
With your mailbox of a jaw.
O Nothing! When I ask what's wrong.
I turn my silence over: an astronomical number.
O, How I could go on!

Market to market I go and come home.
My silence runs parallel to the direction of my travel.
My silence makes a district with just one
constituent. I am the legislator of my mother.

My silence doesn't ask, doesn't eat, doesn't act.
I am sick on it, celibate
and exhausted. Each night
I am up with it: Sublunary Thing! My silence
is an insomnia.

Let's ask the throat what the mouth wants tonight.
I've grown fat on my refusal to say a word. I turn my silence over
and there's a doubling of my mother. I've been doing
little sit-ups with my sense of reserve:

I'll wait. I'll waste my turn. I have my way—my one!
I turn my silence over. I'm not speaking
to my mother. Like God, I guess
I've already come.

Love Is Not a Word

Sweet La
my Dee Da, my daughter's
an idea.

I could break her bready body
from the sweaty blankets of the bed.
I could hold her head.

I would comb her hair.

A dove is not a word, but love
is a lisper.

A telephone is not an ear
but the last time I tried, I could hear
your fear: the egg

in the air. You're the bird,
I'm the bear.

What we did have.
Where we did go.
What we do.

Flu Song in Spanish

God of the bees, god of gold keys, god of all in-
famous noses, I folded our total
in two today—I drove alone
and I walked away (as if each mile up your hill
were a letter in a word I'm inventing).
So I stuck my head in a hole and stood.
So far so. So far
good. Now I wear that hole like a hood
in a house
of inscrutable signals.

God of the guess, god of the gap
mind if I make you a martyr?
If the sky says anything, it's everything! at once!
(Nor did you answer my question.)
So I stick my head in a hole and stand. So far
so far. So far, grand. Sand in my pants and ants
in the box, I wish there were bells
for when I should stop.
Show me the bell for when I should stop!
(Not that I'd know when to ring it.)

Grant me the grace and I'll fix it. Shit.
My father (that bitch!) he hides
at the head
of his third wife's table.
The man says one thing then
nothing. For months.
(Though I've always been welcome to dinner.)
So I stook my head in a hole instead.
So far: slow car: a sofa bed. A brick in the back
where he buries the dead. His task is her
two daughters.

God of the aster, God of disaster, God of
charisma and risk: if a word and a wing
are the same stringy thing
then what in the world can I say?
The sign means too much: you translate
my hunch (there's no chance in hell today).
So I stick my head in a hole and drown. So far
lost, so far I found a bone-cutter's house
in a blood-lit town: I swear I'll tear your eyes away.

THE FOUR CORNERS OF FIFTH & LENORA

I timed my arrival to make an X.
At the intersection you were on the other side.
I smiled like the city bus between us.
A sick, fluorescent smile.
In that moment my coat blew open:
half-slip hiked around my waist,
my hair I hoped a wave of grain. This
is not a weekend feeling.
I am holding my heart against my chest.
In the city of just me I am unanimous.
You must change your life.

Untitled Manifesto

When I met your wife it was
in her kitchen, with dishes.
The kitchen was pitted with bowls.
She looked at me like a mother
entrusting her infant.
Her look had hands in it, hello.
I accepted her infant
like an adolescent. I took it
with instincts for arms.
Later, when I met you at midnight
I was holding her bundle between us.
So you made your approach
from the side and behind.

Fever with Guitars

You sing because you say you get sick if you stop.
You go out for a walk
and the trees make a trail right through you.
Your blue coat wears you and your shoes just barely
bear you left, where the blackberries snatch at your sleeve.
So you're singing when you say the leaves
in the street are the colors of a bus crash,
which is to say, still singing, that it's been raining
the way it's always raining, mainly, more:
the way you want the girl to have already caught you
against a car door.
So you sing to a sound with a similar song
as the words of what you'd say,
invented by Bach, played by Beethoven
and eyed by the red light on the radio
while you ring when the telephone calls
to say the tables are waiting. The tables are waiting.
The tables are tapping their silverware.
The cigarette smokes you and the bicycle
rides you and your glass pitcher pours you
like one last beer. The television tells you
that the girl says she loves you,
right there: on the criss of your double-crossing ears.

Federico & Garcia

Green you know I want you Green I want you
Green I want you blue no Green
I want your Green to mean
high mass of trees and trick bamboo.
Good I want your gas. Night
I want your nurse.
Now I know the consequence: my half-slip
grass skirt. Thistle
give me a stick, muscle my bungalow
Green I want you black and green—my ration of pistachios.
Boast I want your best. I'm boats.
I want the shore—Green Jack
and Jill attack
and kill
the Emperor of Ecuador.
Jade-Green grenade, my luck's
been laid: most Irish
of all bridesmaids. Green butter
in the batter, Green plate
upon the platter, Green song I'll sing
your serenade.
Green I'll dot your double-cross, your eyes
are upside down. Your nation is a face I've seen
the water wants to rise around.
O Green you know I love you Green
by Green I mean engrave me.
What color is that? The color of wax—
my littlest light Green craving.
But Green I've got your filigree: your wife was my idea
my yellow buffet, *my* Green array—
Green, I want Garcia!
But answer me as anyone—sell me the telephone.
Hire me.
Fire me.
Tomorrow I will it alone.

Green pear I'll do your dare, I'll wear
your chandelier. Green guillotine, sweet
nicotine, my mirror,
hang me here.

Intimacy Vs. Autonomy

Light began time.
We filled our daybuckets with it.
We battled our umbrellas.

We dropped our dresses in gutters of gathers.
We managed our fans of poker feathers.

We gave each gust a good hard twist—
invisible sacks of bread on by.
Well! And still. We live like we're hills.

Imagine my mother imagine her father.
Now I'm herding the sky.

Words for the Waltz

All night long I've resisted his help.
What is the opposite of *fast?*

Forcing a kid who's throwing a fit
—you standing thing you never sit!
You'll run us all aground!—Help

has water
just like this: to get us
turned around.
But this kid kicks when you pick her up so

there: throw her down.

* * *

—and we have arrived. We have
arriven. My minions
push down the plank of my neck
and back.

We stand on four legs like a makeshift table
until all hell's dispatched.
So into the itch! Into the thicket!
The careful course is cast.

We make emotional revisitings.
On the hills of impassioned ants.

* * *

Snail snail glister me forward,
bird my back to the wall.
God begot me from my father
and delivered the hospital home.

* * *

All day long I've resisted that red
while I tried to make it match.

I've taken the ax of my effort like a paddle
and I'm hacking at the shadows
of my feet.

I've taken the ax of my effort like a paddle
and I'm dragging this raft
through a lake

made of concrete.

* * *

Oh hell, oh well. Admit
you made a mess.
Now you must tear up the carpet.
Now you must repaint the walls.
The color says nothing but there is a judgment:
everything but the garbage can must go.

* * *

Often stranded in the middle of a feeling the feeling
of wanting so many is more.
Snail snail glister me forward trail the trailing
translucent cord.

* * *

Think of it! A sycophant!
A guttersnipe! A gripe!

Good help has rivers
filled with fish—*sidelong pickerel*

smiles. Would with the river and *would*
with the fish. His red face

the same from behind.

* * *

All day long I've insisted on help.
In the basement
I'm like a bad cramp.
The sun is against me the moon would not have me
my tantrum matches the lamp.

* * *

I've taken
the ax
of my effort
like a paddle
and I'm hacking
at the shadow
of my throat.

I have taken the ax
of my effort
like a paddle
and I'm dragging
this lake

through a hole
in my boat.

* * *

There's a mirror

next to the window and a window
on the wall. Smile, he says
in the middle of the fuss. Eat it.
Now swallow.

* * *

'Twas a lovely dive, my lively dove
What's winter for? To remember love.

Good help has daughters
just like this: "My father
invented water."
God help us daughters just like this:
I with no rights in this matter.

* * *

The body's a closet
with cats in the back.
The sea's grown woolen
and white. I am
his consolable widow
now—one syllable
bigger than wife.

The Curtains Are Another Kind of Husband

Drawn in the daytime, they are grand,
gruff and complete with cuffs. Another kind of

eight-in-all, they are near, but not enough.
The curtains are cryptic and unwilling to billow

when the windows are closed.
They whisper, they whistle, they call me

glaucoma. Clearly they can't speak, clearly
they can't see me, but they do drape

like the arms of an angel-ape
down the sides of each see-through torso.

The curtains make flirting make sense and
make fun. The last one teases me.

My grooms disagree with me and I am both
embarrassed and proud. I am embarrassed

to be so proud, but I am also proud
of this embarrassment. They say

they give me a place, but they take my place.
They take my time and they give way.

Double Down

I try to make a poem in order to be smart
about the way one dog walked
when he wanted to run around.

Look at my dead dog now!

Demonstrated in the slant flight of a seaplane in the sky
where someone is devoting himself
to a direction I recognize.

Smudge of a dog, up and to the west, I try.

Looking to the left while I'm walking
to the right, I move
en masse, as if stuck on a raft
with my enemies.
It gets so awkward inside of me. Look:
now I'm out back, berating the garden.

My umbrella isn't in case but the cause of the worst
rain coming down.

My soul is shaped like a shovel buried in the ground.

Hard Feelings

We have gone to bed like dark socks
and we have woken stiffly
like in-laws, like three English uncles
bunking in the basement of a house
that's been on the market for months now.
I act like my bathrobe is a regular sweater
while these three stand around in suits, looking
aimlessly about the basement,
faking their search for who
knows what in which language: three men
turned whither, turned west, and one
watching another face first into the dark drain
of an even darker door.
I might say that I am
in the basement, based on this basementy feeling.
Every morning, I drink
one cup of coffee while the same young couple
checks the kitchen for corners.
My men are pretending intently, without
any extra bending,
hoping for some nook or cranny to plumb, some
crook or nanny dumb enough to tell them what.

Because Because

Because I have both the head
and the hand holding the head
by the hair
I've cut myself a wig and I will sit

as if I had a porch
as if I had a rocking chair.

* * *

Our sex gave way to more sex
then less. As if
every question had an answer asking
yes?

Each mile was a mill.
Each mile was a million.
Every hill was a hell.
One bell was a billion.

The whisker of did
was what one does.
I killed the cat
just because.

Can Be Jackets, Can Be Bees

Skinny Superstitious Leaf-Eating Lady
You plant a box of Brown Flowers by the Black Feet
of an African Jesus
suffering by your Front Door.

You think you've Lost Your Keys. You think
an Early Frost into the Trees and I sit

amid a frizz of crucifixes on the kitchen floor.

Skinny Victimized Venomous Witch
You trip on your tiptoes across my kitchen.
You Sing a Song in fake Chinese:
Can be Jackets, Can be Bees!

Mincing Wincing Tick-Eyed Tease,
your Mystery made the worst of me.

The Clock stopped
and Our Combination Locked
at Four
on the Fourteenth
of February.

Now I keep my teeth
tight, Night
a Gown around my Neck, my Feet
tucked in a sock and the sock
tacked to a tree.

You stalked me with your Babytalk while you stuck me
with your Father's Cock. You Laid
Blame, and I took it
like a thing. I took it
like a Drink from a Glass of gasoline—

(now even
the Garden
is Glaring.)

But Malingering Bringer, just Bring me
a Crust. Much as I love her, I must
muster my lust. She lost
her luster, but I miss
her fuss. And much as I miss her, I miss her
even more.

My love is a hundred black Labradors barking hard at her back door.

The Four Corners of Fifth & Lenora

I timed my arrival to make an X.
At the intersection you were on the other side.
I smiled like the city bus between us.
A sick, fluorescent smile.
In that moment my coat blew open:
half-slip hiked around my waist, my hair I hoped
a wave of grain. This
is not a weekend feeling.
I am holding my heart against my chest.
In the city of history I am still happening.
Goddamn-motherfucking-son-of-a-Bitch!

Pick It Up Again

The end of an insistent autumn. Each tree
the obvious culprit of its yellow litterings.
The girl cutting two blonde braids off her bound head:
careful, careful to let each hank drop
directly into her dresser drawer.
Then the mother out of nowhere, and the girl
with less hair, confused by the trouble
given all the care she took to keep the floor clean.

How can winter mean anything
but desolation? Branches bony as the girl's hand
right where the father dropped it. The fact
of that hand and the father
feet ahead, composing a love poem for his next wife
while the girl waits, rooted in her red boots.
What was conversation is silent: the leaves fall
as if all at once, in bruise-colored clots and rings.

Good God

He asked for the Brahms
and he asked me to translate
each note into English and then speak it
in Braille. Stand still, he said. Stand
here, he said. Go get me a glass of water.
He asked for the Brahms
and he asked for my hands.
He told me to hold them
as if I were counting:
one foot there and the other up
near my ear—balance, balance—now bring me the Brahms.
Then he caught my hips in the camber of his hips
like carlights lost in the bends of a road.
I have called you, he said, by the hairs
on your head. Steady now. Stay there.
Bring me the Brahms.

If English

If geography is the highway I take to your house,
then geology is the house, the cliff it sits on,
the cross hairs the frames cast on the yellow walls.
Geometry is the windows into the living room
and entomology is the key under the brick by the back door.
Biology, then, is the bathroom,
and the shower with you singing inside it
a lecture on erosion in a conservation class.
Chemistry is the kitchen, the feta cheese on the counter,
and how many leaves is calculus
collected in the corner by the pot of wilted daffodils.
The brother's abandoned bedroom is history: his globe,
his football helmet, his ratty blue bathrobe.
And if the front porch is philosophy
with eye-screws in the rafters where a swing should be,
then theology is the front door ajar.
In English I'd say English
is the telephone and the telephone book
and the table with one vase and the cut rose.
Belief would be the unmade bed
and any discussion of God, your body
still sleeping beside your clothes.

The Time Eater

She's not
just a cat or a cat's color black, not a number
of rings or rounds.
All the yeslets in their nests must
yes, acquiesce: silence
knows the sound.

She's sitting like a cistern beside me.
For silence knows how long.
The counter-clock,
unraveling, makes a tick
like her chittering crowtalk.

Less cat than cut, she's a dark
remark, a nap
underneath a piano: the drain
whole days
like money
and rain
and the plural
of down

is again.
The drain.
Whole days.
Money and rain.
Silence makes
a mean companion.

The Chief

When what has helped us
has helped us enough and knows it
and walks away
with her backpack over one shoulder,
then what will want us
will sit opposite on the other couch.
What will take us
will practice tennis at night
while we sit in the dark inhabited house, heat on
and all the windows open,
each car driving by driving hard
up the hill.

When what has held us
has held us harder than we wanted
and who we thought we heard knocking
was knocking
but on the neighbor's door,
then what has harmed us will hold
what has helped us
like one egg in a very small bowl.

I am standing at the dirt grave of one buried Indian chief.
My love has brought me to this cemetery in the cold.

When what will hold us loosely,
with one hand on the back of our neck
does have her hand there
and keeps it,
even while we bend down
to stab a scrap of a poem
into the weeds where the chief's chest should be,
then what has helped us says enough.

It is the first moment of midnight in the exact middle of winter.
My love has brought me to this cemetery in the cold.
We stand very still for just one minute and then I'm ready to go.

THE WRONG PLACE FOR A LONG TIME

When I ask if she wants to start running at the farthest fir tree,
she guesses, hedges her bets, she asks *what?*
and means yes.
Another number adds one to itself
and we call it an accumulation of tenderness:
She will need me and I will need her to need me and not
the other way around,
resembling nothing much more than love, even now.
Nothing much that I can tell.
Not an alcoholic and not

not an alcoholic, we spend every Sunday discussing what
each of us meant by what we said to the other, forever
getting ready to be able to begin to say
what neither of us will let
just yet. Not a lot unlike building a bridge in a cartoon:
nailing the one plank, then stepping out
to nail the next, dividing the *good bye* from the *by*
god, the big *if* from the bullheaded *but,* always leaving
and always about to leave: *lervous,*
by which I mean *a little nervous* and she will understand.

EACH FOOT AS FEET SHOULD

I say blue
but what I mean is
blonde braids
bleaching on the beach, one straw stuck
in a waxed paper cup,
her name the way her hair hangs
and how she holds her shoulders high
between the tight sleeves
of her white blouse. Blue
but with salt
and the sound of one boat
dragging its anchor just offshore.

I say church
and I wait.
What I get is a white face
conflicted with the signs of the cross
like trees
constricted with the first frost
on the streets of the walk I take
so often it's not a walk
but where I pace,
where I watch the moon
like my own blemished face
and then the moon again
like the memory of my left hand
slapping a glass of water across a tabletop.

We're at the coast. The water is here
and the gulls and white boats.
The sand is trashed with children.

I watch the water break
on a boat and I know:
the closest you can get to the ocean

is to get into it.
And all day her body
has been the only body
on the beach:
legs like
her legs.
The small of her back
small as the small of her back
can be. Wet hair the color of her hair
wet, the color of cut wood. And her feet:
both her feet
just like two feet should.

Head of a Girl

A boy presses one knee on his sister's ribs, spits
and sucks and spits again.
The father in another room holds headphones
on his red ears, country music
loud enough for the girl to hear.
When the wife touches his shoulder
he aims for an eye, spits
and he hits it. She walks away, calls the kids
cuts four steaks on white plates and sits.

Just like that: the mother drops the girl
on the edge of town.

The girl presses against a twin bed,
tracing the ribs on a pale strange bedspread.
Her aunt says God won't give you more than you
can take.

Nothing. Not even water that week.

Years: a desert, the grandmother
dies. There's the bird
the girl starves and buries in a coffee can,
a man, his thermos of gin, twin

hospital beds under thin ribbed spreads
guarded by brick bridge rails.
She scrapes her name in water

on a wet step and forgets it. No matter
what weather, she keeps her fingerprints
pressed inside a pair of gray gloves.

THE MEAN TIME

After San Francisco, after getting back
from going to San Francisco,
I wash one glass while I unpack
and collect the half-eaten apples
of the afternoon I left
all afternoon. All through each room
of the intolerable tract house of the afternoon:
the interim of the airplane,
the interrogation of the seat strap, then out
into the bright humiliation of high noon.
I'm back to the embarrassment of the bathroom
where the one window watches
while I tweeze tiny feathers
from the breast of the bath mat between
twelve and two. I can feel my feet
because I can feel my feet on fire.
Burnt to the slack asphalt
of the black tarmac
staunching the center of the living room.
I am burning because I've been built to burn
and I have been burning
because I've been left to burn
and I am still burning,
built like a boat tied to a float
and I am forbidden to turn.

Chicken

You bite at the side of your mouth and I think
scissors in a fist fight and foxglove

wrestling a red fence.
Your mouth

is a month.
I'm across the river.

Stuck on a rock in the middle of
November–

weather-fed a rolling freight of firewood.
You say one

three word thing
like an accident of birds

startled from a farm tree.
Your eyes

like eyes look
then your eyes

like tracks. I'm fixing
a chicken still digging for scratch.

Letter from One Less Daughter

I've been working hard at keeping the house clean,
books battened in the tall shelves,
letters in their order. I've been working hard at
working hard and the work gets done
in great shoves, each room tidied when I leave it.

You love more than me.
Maybe you love my father, his hand
on my shoulder, his high
family forehead: his eyes are like a sum.
Maybe you love my discomfort
standing on the tree stump.
My loneliness,
you must love it
as you must love everyone.

But tell me if I read this right:
when I slipped on the rock cliff above the river, I took a hawk
wheeling in yellow leaves as a sign reading
should I leave her?

I am so sick of myself.

The Four Corners of Fifth & Lenora

So I timed my arrival to make an X.
At the intersection you were on the other side.
I smiled like the city bus between us.
A sick, fluorescent smile.
In that moment my coat blew open—
half-slip hiked around my waist,
my hair I hoped a wave of grain. This
is not a weekend feeling.
I am holding my heart against my chest.
In the city of just me I am unanimous.
You know who you are.

(NOTES)

p. vi: The poem "American Husband" borrows its tune from The Guess Who's "American Woman." The poem also takes from Sylvia Plath's "Daddy" and Emily Dickinson's 156.

p. 1: Thanks again to Olena, who invented the idea of this poem four times, each with different endings. The last lines on this first version are mine. Also, thanks to Kevin: you know who you are.

p. 2: "More of the Same" owes itself to a haiku by Basho: "Even in Kyoto— / hearing the cuckoo's cry— / I long for Kyoto."

p. 3: "Cruelty Made Me" borrows most of its first line from Linda Gregg's "The Limits of Desire" and its title from her "Etiology." Thanks, Linda Gregg. (sorry!)

p. 9: "I Turn My Silence Over" includes and combines ideas from the Sunni poet Shajahana's "A Rainbow" (translated by Syamala Kallury and R. Parthasarathy), Sylvia Plath's "A Birthday Present," Brenda Shaughnessey's "Why Is the Color of Snow," Mother Goose, and Orhan Pamuk's *The Black Book*.

p. 15: In this version of "The Four Corners of Fifth & Lenora," the last line is Rilke's, from his "The Archaic Torso of Apollo," Stephen Mitchell, translator.

p. 18: "Federico & Garcia" is based on the repeating first line of Federico Garcia Lorca's "Sleepwalkers' Ballad."

p. 21: "Words for the Waltz" is a poem which was commissioned for "The Roethke Readings," a celebration of Theodore Roethke's work. The poem's italicized lines are all Roethke's. The manner in which I made the poem was/is his as well.

p. 26: "Double Down" is for Easy the dog.

p. 27: "Hard Feelings" is based on a drawing by Edward Gorey. The caption underneath the drawing reads, "They searched the cellar Fruitlessly."

p. 28: "Because Because" owes itself to *The Wizard of Oz*'s "We're Off to See the Wizard."

p. 29: Love you, Trisha!

p. 31: In this version of "Four Corners," the last line is my mother's, from memory.

p. 34: "If English" is modeled on Li-Young Lee's "This Room and Everything in It."

p. 36: "The Chief" is based on W. S. Merwin's line, "When what has helped us has helped us enough."

p. 41: "Each Foot as Feet Should" is heavily influenced by Jack Gilbert's "The Forgotten Dialect of The Heart." This poem is for Jessica.

p. 42: The structure of "The Mean Time" borrows from parts of T. S. Eliot's "Ash Wednesday."

p. 45: The last line of this version of this poem was (inadvertently[!?]) STOLEN from the last line of Kevin Craft's "Linear A." Thanks, Jarvin!